FOLLOW CHESTER!

A College Football Team Fights Racism *and* Makes History

Charlesbridge

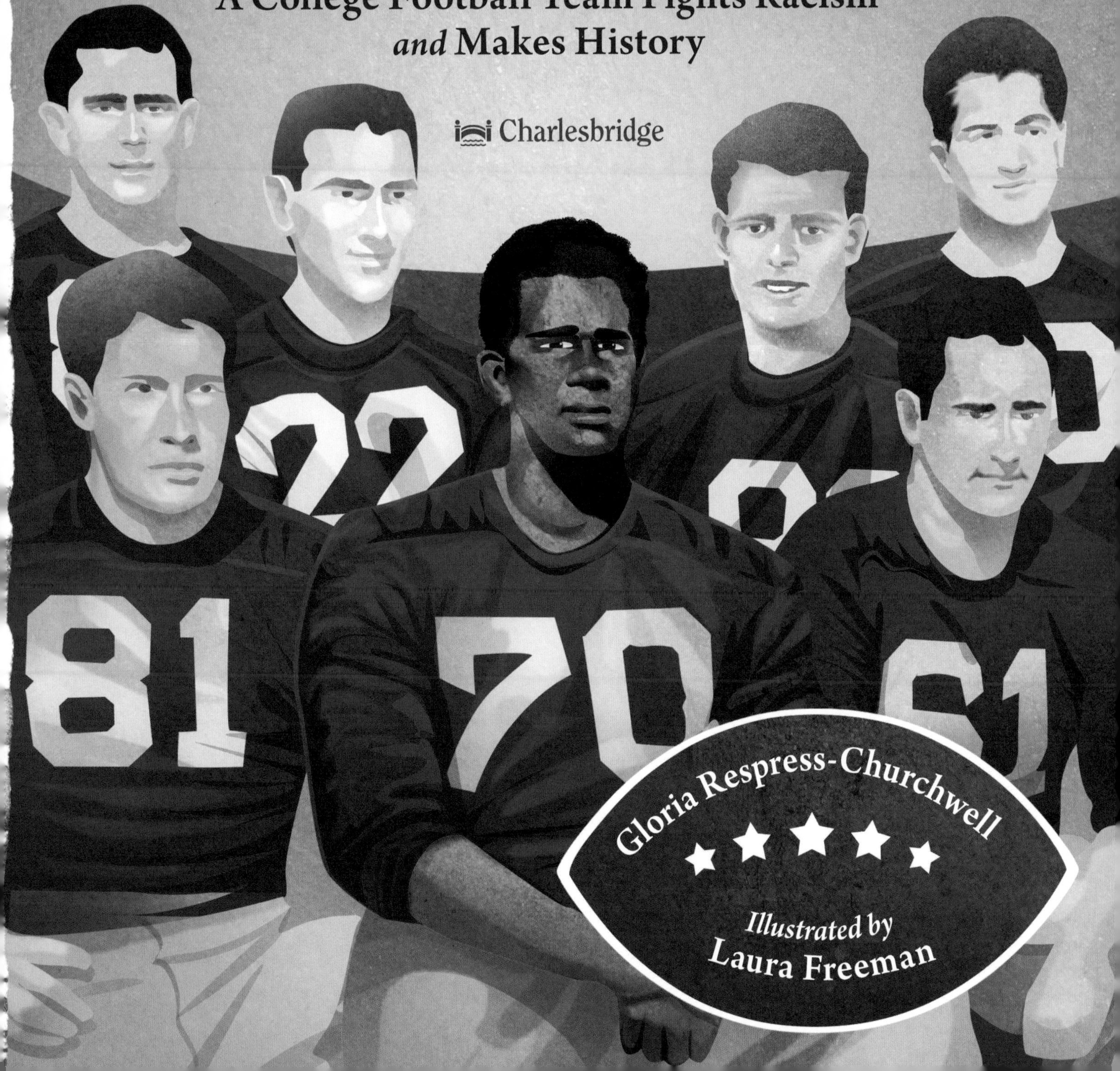

Gloria Respress-Churchwell

Illustrated by
Laura Freeman

To my supportive family, who inspired me to keep following where Chester's story led—G. R. C.

For Angel (Jacqui)—L. F.

Acknowledgments

Sincere appreciation to the Pierce family; my editor, Karen Boss; the Harvard Athletics Department; UVA librarian Barbara Selby; Simmons Writers Encouraged (WE!) Critique Group; Megan Lambert; and Dr. Cathryn Mercier.

At the time of publication, all URLs printed in this book were accurate and active. Charlesbridge, the author, and the illustrator are not responsible for the content or accessibility of any website.

Published by Charlesbridge
85 Main Street
Watertown, MA 02472
(617) 926-0329
www.charlesbridge.com

Library of Congress Cataloging-in-Publication Data
Names: Respress-Churchwell, Gloria, author.
Title: Follow Chester!: a college football team fights racism and makes history /
    Gloria Respress-Churchwell; illustrated by Laura Freeman.
Description: Watertown, MA : Charlesbridge, [2019]
Identifiers: LCCN 2018037908 (print) | LCCN 2018060225 (ebook) |
    ISBN 9781632897237 (ebook) | ISBN 9781632897244 (ebook pdf) |
    ISBN 9781580898355 (reinforced for library use)
Subjects: LCSH: Pierce, Chester M. | Football players—United States—Biography.
    | Psychiatrists—United States—Biography. | Harvard University—Football—
    History. | College sports—United States—History. | College sports—Social
    aspects—United States. | Racism in sports—United States—History. |
    Discrimination in sports—United States—History.
Classification: LCC GV939.P53 (ebook) | LCC GV939.P53 R47 2019 (print) |
    DDC 796.332092 [B]—dc23
LC record available at https://lccn.loc.gov/2018037908

Printed in China
(hc) 10 9 8 7 6 5 4 3 2 1

Illustrations done in Photoshop
Display type set in Ivy League by Swfte International
Text type set in Arno Pro by Adobe Systems Incorporated
Color separations by Colourscan Print Co Pte Ltd, Singapore
Printed by 1010 Printing International Limited in Huizhou, Guangdong, China
Production supervision by Brian G. Walker
Designed by Diane M. Earley

One summer when Chester Pierce was about eight,
his younger brother fell down a well.

Chester quickly threw down
a chain, and with a friend's help,
pulled his brother up. News traveled
fast in the small town of Glen Cove,
New York, about Chester's brave act.
He became a local hero.

But Chester still lacked confidence. He felt like he was too skinny, and he definitely didn't think he was as handsome as his two brothers.

Chester loved football, basketball, and music. He played the piano, accordion, and trumpet. He became his high school's first black senior-class president. Chester applied to Harvard University with encouragement from his teacher. The principal doubted he'd get in, but Chester had to try. With hard work, he was accepted.

His confidence grew.

WHITE

COLORED

HARVARD
FOOTBALL SCHEDULE 1947

DATE	OPPONENT
SEPT 27	W. MARYLAND
OCT 4	BOSTON U
OCT 11	VIRGINIA
OCT 25	DARTMOUTH
NOV 1	RUTGERS
NOV 8	PRINCETON
NOV 15	BROWN
NOV 18	HOLY CROSS
NOV 22	YALE

Chester played varsity football at Harvard. His team was scheduled to play the University of Virginia (UVA) in Charlottesville, Virginia. It was 1947, and colleges in the South didn't allow black students. Jim Crow laws kept black and white people separate. The UVA coaches thought Harvard wouldn't bring Chester.

But Jackie Robinson had just broken the color barrier to become the first black person on a major league baseball team. Harvard knew that the United States was slowly changing. Chester's coach pulled him aside and said, "Get ready. You're going with us to UVA. You deserve to play."

Chester understood that being the first black person to do something was never easy. Jackie Robinson had been spat on and called horrible names. At Harvard, Chester was called names by some white students. He didn't let that stop him.

He thought about what his coach said about deserving to play. He had to stay confident.

Chester's teammates understood he was nervous. They wanted to help.

"We're with you, Chester, no matter what," one teammate said.

"Jim Crow laws are wrong!" another teammate said. Someone else threw down his helmet.

"People shouldn't try to divide us. We're one team," another protested.

Chester knew the best way to fight was with his mind. He had an idea about how to stand up to racism.

"Let's create a special play for on and off the field. Whenever we use the play, it means we act as one," Chester said.

"Great idea. Let's call it 'Follow Chester!'" someone called out.

Chester and his teammates shook hands. The play was in place.

The night before they left for Virginia, Chester was still uneasy. He knew talking to his mother would help.

She listened and replied, "I know you'll do your best, Chester. If your dad were still alive, he would want you to stare down all adversity with courage."

The bus ride to UVA was long. Chester gazed out the
window as the bus crossed the Mason-Dixon Line—the
cultural boundary between North and South.

MASON-DIXO

Made famous as line
free and slave state
War between the Sta
survey establishing M
Pennsylvania boundar
1763; halted by Indi
1767; continued to so
corner, 1782; marke

The Harvard bus pulled into a service station late in the evening. Chester and his teammates came face to face with a restroom sign that read "Whites Only."

They needed to use the bathroom. They stood uncomfortably on one foot, then on the other. Chester started walking towards the woods.

Someone yelled, "Follow Chester!"

If Chester couldn't use the bathroom, none of them would.

The Virginia coach met the bus. "We thought you wouldn't bring the black player. He can't sleep in any hotel. And he's sure not staying here," he said to the Harvard coach.

Chester and his teammates heard every word.

Chester's coach wouldn't take no for an answer, and neither would the team. After a lot of pressure, UVA provided housing for Chester. His teammates stayed with him. They stood together.

Another roadblock appeared the next morning. Black people weren't allowed through the front door of restaurants in Charlottesville. Chester led the march around to the back of the restaurant.

"Follow Chester!" the players shouted. White patrons watched through the windows with open mouths.

COLORED
ENTRANCE

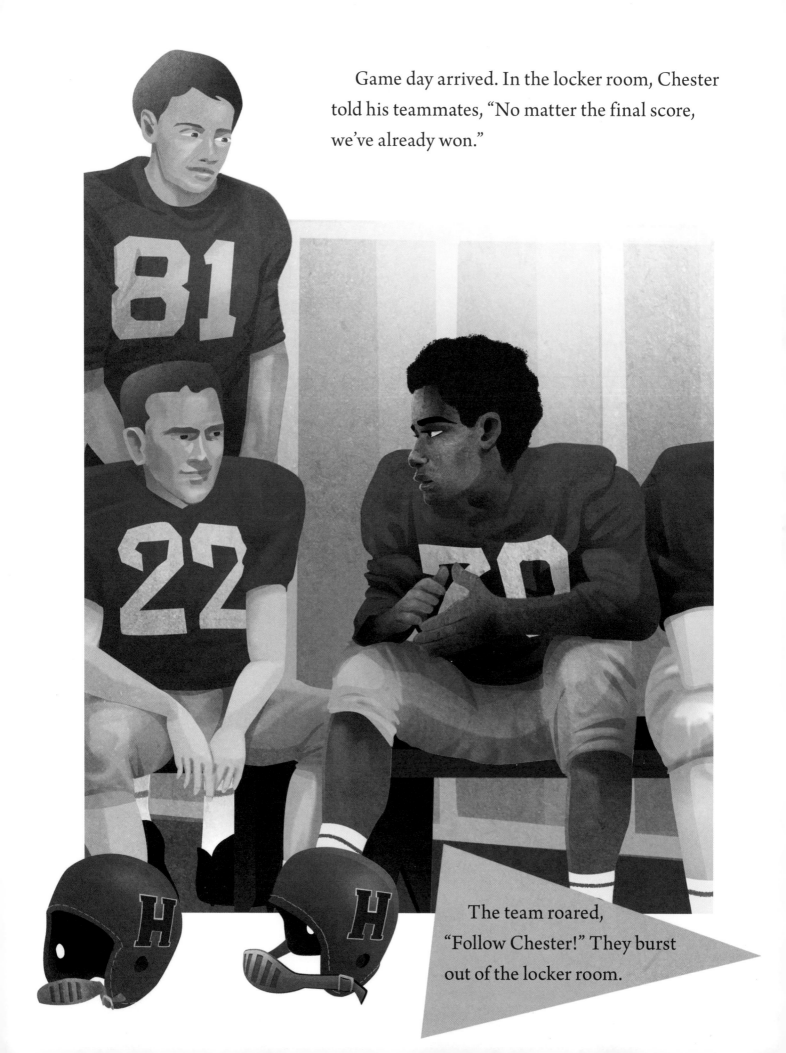

Game day arrived. In the locker room, Chester told his teammates, "No matter the final score, we've already won."

The team roared, "Follow Chester!" They burst out of the locker room.

The stadium was full. The first black player was about to
play against the University of Virginia on their home turf.
Even *Time* magazine showed up to cover the historic game.
Black fans sat in a segregated section—they applauded as
Harvard came onto the field. But many UVA fans booed.

Chester's jersey—number 70—gently flapped
in the wind. He and his teammates marched to
the center of the field. The breeze was at
their backs. There were faint cheers
and some horrible shouts.

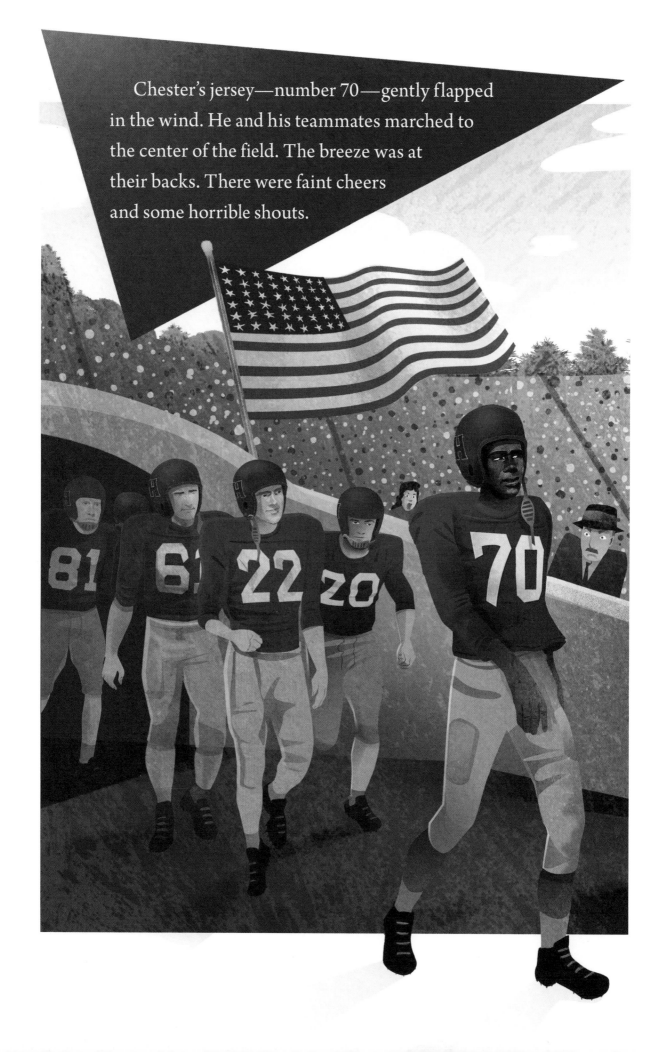

Chester turned and faced the black crowd. He looked up at the clear, blue sky. He thought about his family and his team. Chester raised his right hand proudly as he saluted the black fans. They stood and clapped even louder.

Chester took a deep breath.

Confidence.

Chester crouched on defense. He looked into the eyes of the huge offensive lineman.

"You got some nerve coming here, you—" the offensive lineman started to say.

Tweeeeeeeeeeet! The referee's whistle blew.

The lineman stepped forward, thrusting his shoulders. With perfect timing, Chester faked a move to the right and one to the left. The player plunged— face first—into the grass, and Chester stood over him.

The game went on and on.
UVA had a big lead over Harvard
with only seconds left. Before the UVA
quarterback could complete a pass, Chester grabbed
him and plunged him to the ground with a hard thud.
The black fans and the Harvard sideline cheered!
But the whistle blew. The game was over.

Chester Pierce—with confidence—made history
that day. Harvard lost, but courage stood up to adversity.
That was the real victory.

AUTHOR'S NOTE

After talking with Dr. Chester Pierce and discussing his life with him, I wrote this story. The details about Chester's childhood, college years, how collegiate football worked, the restaurant scene, and Chester's response to the black fans are based on actual events. I changed some details and invented the dialogue, bathroom scene, and the play called "Follow Chester" to create a sense of what it might have been like for him to travel to and play in the South while Jim Crow laws were in place.

Charles Follis, known as "The Black Cyclone," was the first black professional football player (with the Shelby Blues from 1902 to 1906). Fritz Pollard and Bobby Marshall were the first black players in what is now the National Football League (NFL); they played in 1920. In 1933 NFL owners decided that there would be no more African American players. This lockout is attributed to George Preston Marshall, who became owner of the Boston Braves (later the Washington Redskins) in 1932. Marshall refused African American players, and he pressured the league to maintain the same policy.

A breakthrough occurred in 1946, when Cleveland's NFL team, the Rams, moved to Los Angeles and wanted to play at the Los Angeles Memorial Coliseum. The LA Dons, from the All-American Football Conference (AAFC), also applied. The Coliseum Commission and black sportswriters (*Los Angeles Tribune* sports editor Halley Harding in particular) pushed the NFL to integrate as a condition of the lease. Both the Rams and the Dons announced they would. Kenny Washington and Woody Strode signed with the Rams. In the same year, Bill Willis and Marion Motley signed and played for the Cleveland Browns.

Even though professional football was integrated, colleges in the South didn't allow black players until the 1960s. Black students who wanted to play football usually went to historically black colleges and universities (HBCUs) such as Grambling State and Jackson State.

Chester Pierce made history in 1947. UVA thought Harvard would sit Chester out and expected they wouldn't bring him at all. There was an unwritten college-football agreement that said when integrated college football teams played schools in the South, they wouldn't play their black players. The all-white Southern team chose a player of equal talent to sit out the game.

When Jackie Robinson broke the baseball color barrier in 1947, Harvard knew history was on their side.

An article in the *Harvard Crimson* said, "Virginia officials scheduled the game hoping Harvard would voluntarily exclude Pierce. But Crimson Athletic Director Bill Bingham insisted on Pierce's participation, and Virginia relented."

Many newspapers and magazines covered the game. *Boston Globe* journalist Jeremiah Murphy (who was a UVA student at the time) described a significant moment: "Chet Pierce turned and faced the segregated black crowd behind the end zone. He was about 6-feet-3 and 235 pounds. He stood there for a second and then held up his right hand and saluted the black crowd. They stood up and applauded."

Dr. Chester Pierce always said he didn't do anything special. I have never spoken with a humbler man, especially given all his vast accomplishments. Although Dr. Pierce passed away in September 2016, his family and I talked, and they are pleased about this book.

Dr. Pierce's courageous story can speak to all of us: *Adversity develops courage! Confidence lives in each of us!* My hope is that *Follow Chester!* will inspire young readers to seek out additional information about Dr. Pierce and other such heroes.

FACTS ABOUT THE MASON-DIXON LINE

- Charles Mason and Jeremiah Dixon drew the Mason-Dixon Line between 1763 and 1767 to mark the boundary between the North and South of the United States. The line borders Pennsylvania, Maryland, Delaware, and the western part of Virginia.
- In the early 1800s the Mason-Dixon Line represented freedom for those escaping slavery in the South. Once they made it over the Mason-Dixon Line, black people were considered free and safe from slave catchers. But that changed in 1850 with the Fugitive Slave Act. Then slave owners were allowed to capture their former slaves no matter where they escaped.
- During the Jim Crow era (from the 1870s through the 1950s), the Mason-Dixon Line represented the difference between the North (a more tolerant part of the country for black people) and the South (a place where the laws still granted fewer rights to black people than white people).
- Today many prejudices still exist. Racism excludes people from education, jobs, housing, medical care, political power, and other opportunities. The spirit of Dr. Pierce and his teammates can inspire each of us to work together to bring about change.

FACTS ABOUT DR. CHESTER PIERCE AND THE HISTORIC GAME AT UVA

- Chester Middlebrook Pierce, known as Chet, was born in Glen Cove, New York, in 1927, to Samuel Pierce and Hettie Pierce. He had two brothers, Burton and Samuel.
- Chester played varsity football, lacrosse, and basketball while at Harvard.
- Robert F. Kennedy was a teammate (#86). He was unable to go with the team to the UVA game because he broke his leg in practice.
- *Time* magazine documented a crowd of 24,000 at the historic game on October 11, 1947. UVA beat Harvard 47–0.
- Some 60 years later, the University of Virginia awarded Dr. Pierce the Vivian Pinn Distinguished Lecturer Award to honor his medical achievements and his lifetime of work on health disparities.
- After graduating from Harvard in 1948, Chester attended Harvard Medical School and became a psychiatrist. He was involved in research in Antarctica and with NASA.
- Chester coined the term "microaggression" in the 1970s. Used widely today, it refers to the everyday insults and dismissals that people of color endure in the United States.
- He lectured on all seven continents and worked in dozens of countries.
- Pierce Peak in Antarctica is named for him.
- Dr. Pierce studied NFL players' behaviors around competition and the effects of fatigue and stress.
- Joan Cooney, the creator of *Sesame Street*, invited Dr. Pierce to help plan the show as an expert consultant.

BIBLIOGRAPHY

Interviews and Correspondence

Dr. Chester Pierce, emeritus professor of education and psychiatry at Harvard Medical School. Personal interviews, 2014 and 2015.

Dr. Alvin Poussaint, friend and colleague of Chester Pierce and professor of psychiatry at Harvard Medical School, writes widely about child psychiatry with a particular focus on raising African American children. Personal correspondence, 2016 and 2017.

Books

Appiah, Kwame Anthony and Henry Louis Gates. *Africana: The Encyclopedia of the African and African American Experience.* New York: Basic Civitas, 1999.

Griffith, Ezra E. H. *Race & Excellence: My Dialogue with Chester Pierce.* University of Iowa Press, 1998.

Articles and Reports

"New Faces," *Harvard Magazine* (January–February 2011). http://harvardmagazine.com/2011/01/new-faces

Fiftieth Anniversary Report of the Harvard College Class of 1948. Chester Pierce entry. Cambridge, 1998.

Gewertz, Ken. "Against All Odds." *Harvard Gazette*, November 18, 2004. http://news.harvard.edu/gazette/story/2004/11/against-all-odds/

"Harvardman Pierce Applause in the South" (National Affairs). *Time*, 20 October 1947, 25.

Murphy, Jeremiah. "Some Stories Stay with You," *Boston Globe*. June 2, 1981.

"24,000 Fans Expected to View Crimson—Orange and Blue Tilt." *College Topics*. University of Virginia. October 21, 1947.

Websites

Harvard University, Football. "Chester M. Pierce Made History on the Field and in the Classroom." http://gocrimson.com/sports/fball/2010-11/releases/101007_Chester_Pierce_NCAA

Massachusetts General Hospital Global Psychiatry, About Us. "Chester Pierce." http://www.mghglobalpsychiatry.org/chesterpierce.php

The Undefeated, Black Achievement. Miller, Jeff. "Harvard's Chester Pierce was Trailblazer in His Field and On the Field." https://theundefeated.com/features/harvards-chester-pierce-was-trailblazer-in-his-field-and-on-the-field/

NFL Ops, Football Operations. "The Reintegration of the NFL." http://operations.nfl.com/the-players/evolution-of-the-nfl-player/the-reintegration-of-the-nfl/

SOURCE NOTES

p. 18: "The Virginia coach met the bus." Griffith, p. 32. Ezra E. H. Griffith, professor emeritus of psychiatry and African American studies, Yale University, noted in his book: "The southern institution made it clear that he couldn't stay in the same hotel with his teammates; but in a conciliatory gesture, the university still provided a mansion where he could sleep."

p. 21: "Another roadblock appeared." Griffith, p. 32. "The [Harvard] coach and the team stood by [Chester] and they all went through the kitchen with their beleaguered teammate."

p. 25: "Chester turned and faced the crowd." Murphy. Jeremiah Murphy was a UVA student who attended the historic football game. As a *Boston Globe* columnist, he wrote about the game years later: "[Chester] stood there for a second and then held up his right hand and saluted the black crowd. They stood up and applauded."

Harvard Crimson football team, 1947 starting line, including Chester Pierce, number 70, and Robert Francis Kennedy, number 86.

COURTESY OF HARVARD ATHLETICS